10 Little Hot Dogs

Written and illustrated by

John Himmelman

two lions

two lions

For James and Madigan
—J.H.

Text and illustrations copyright © 2010 by John Himmelman

Amazon Publishing
Attn: Amazon Children's Publishing
P.O. Box 400818, Las Vegas, NV 89140
www.amazon.com/amazonchildrenspublishing

Library of Congress Cataloging-in-Publication Data
Himmelman, John.
10 little hot dogs / John Himmelman. — 1st ed.
p. cm.
Summary: One by one, ten excitable dachshunds pile onto a chair.
ISBN 978-1-4778-1075-0
[1. Dachshunds—Fiction. 2. Dogs—Fiction. 3. Counting.] I. Title. II.
Title: Ten little hot dogs.
PZ7.H5684Aag 2010
[E]—dc22
2009042307

The illustrations are rendered in watercolor and lines drawn with black Prismacolor pencil.
Book design by Anahid Hamparian
Editor: Robin Benjamin
Printed in China

1 One little hot dog sitting on a chair . . .

"I want a friend to sit with me!"

2 Two little hot dogs sitting on a chair . . .

"There's more room on the pillow!"

3 Three little hot dogs sitting on a chair . . .

"We want a bone to chew!"

4 Four little hot dogs wagging on a chair . . .

"Let's play catch!"

5

Five little hot dogs playing on a chair . . .

"We want a sock to tug!"

6 Six little hot dogs bouncing on a chair . . .

"How about a shoe?"

7 Seven little hot dogs tumbling on a chair . . .

"Now we need a hat!"

8

Eight little hot dogs jumping on a chair . . .

"Don't forget the blanket!"

9 Nine little hot dogs scattered on a chair . . .

"We need one more dog for the dog pile!
Whew, we're tired."

10 Ten little hot dogs all fast asleep.
Shhhhh . . .

Uh-oh . . .

9

Nine little hot dogs still fast asleep.
Shhhhh . . .

8 **Eight little hot dogs still fast asleep.**
Shhhhh . . .

7 Seven little hot dogs still fast asleep.
Shhhhh . . .

6 Six little hot dogs still fast asleep.
Shhhhh . . .

5

Five little hot dogs still fast asleep.
Shhhhh . . .

4 Four little hot dogs still fast asleep. *Shhhhh . . .*

3 **Three little hot dogs still fast asleep.**
Shhhhh . . .

2 **Two little hot dogs still fast asleep.**
Shhhhh . . .

1

One little hot dog still fast asleep.
Shhhhh . . .

1 **One little hot dog wide awake.**
"Hey, you little hot dogs, wake up and play!"